IMPORTANT: READ FIRST!

# A MESSAGE FROM THE PUBLISHER

Dear Reader:

Sorry to delay the opening of this book, but it has come to our attention (in other words, the author has been ranting, raving, and carrying on like the world is coming to an end) that the following facts are not about pigs after all.

According to her, they're about FIGS.

Not to make excuses, but we don't really know how to explain the mix-up. Chalk it up to one of those eensy-teensy "boo-boos" (as we say in the business). Look, mistakes happen. The "F" looked like a "P," okay?

We told the author, "Lighten up, let it go." What did she expect us to do? Scrap the whole book because of a little mishap with ONE letter?

Besides, everyone here thinks the book works fine just the way it is. Pigs? Figs? No biggie.

Of course, the author (a.k.a. drama queen), being one of those "writer types" (oh boy, could we tell you stories about how that bunch acts up when their words are changed), insisted (translated: threatened legal action) that we add this note.

So, here it is:

The book is about Figs. Not Pigs.

Again, to our readers out there—we think it all works!

So . . . enjoy!

Signed,

*Hamilton A. Cochon*

Hamilton A. Cochon
Publisher and Executive Editor

M.P.—There you go. All fixed. Happy now?
—H. A. C.

NO!
—M.P.

written by
Margie Palatini

illustrated by
Chuck Groenink

ABRAMS BOOKS FOR YOUNG READERS
NEW YORK

# UNDER A ~~PIG~~ TREE

## A History of the Noble Fruit

# FIG!

## FIGS! IT'S FIGS, I TELL YOU!

Pigs appear in the earliest recorded history.

Pigs were presented as "medals" to the winners of the first Olympics in 776 BC.

Every citizen of ancient Athens, including Plato, was called "A Friend of the Pig."

Figs, people. These are facts about FIGS!

It was pigs, as well as the famous asp in the basket, that were delivered to Cleopatra back in 30 BC.

*Are you kidding?*
*— M.P.*

Pigs were found everywhere during the time of the Roman Empire and were seen frequently throughout China's Ming Dynasty.

Charlemagne introduced the pig to the Netherlands in AD 812, but unfortunately the pig was not able to adapt to cold weather.

Seriously? — M.P.

Today, however, pigs are found all over the globe.
There are Mediterranean pigs. Turkish pigs.

Have you people lost

Pigs are in Australia, Chile, Bengal, Egypt, and Italy,
and many can be found in Texas, Oregon, and, of course,
California, which is famous for the Mission Pig.

your minds?!!—M.P.

Some pigs are very popular and quite famous, such as Blanche, Celeste, Len, and Tena. Of course, everyone knows Judy.

Most pigs thrive
in a full day of sun.

Full day?
Please check
for accuracy.
H.A.C.

They love a hot, dry summer and a cool, moist winter.

Some pigs can be delicate, so please do protect them from frost!

ME check for accuracy?

Nothing is better than a pig right
off a tree. Look for the ones on low
branches. They droop a bit but feel nice
and soft, and are not mushy.

Nobody is
buying this!!
—M.P.

However, be careful, as most pigs tend to become spoiled.

Dear M.P.,
Do you see how unattractive acting like a spoiled child can be?
H.A.C.

EXCUSE ME?!

Today, pigs are extremely popular with celebrity gourmet chefs. They are frequently found in the best and most glamorous restaurants.

But pigs can be simple and hearty, too.

I'm calling my agent. —M.P.

And, of course, there is nothing better than enjoying a hot cup of tea or a cold glass of milk with one of those famous Pig Newtons.

Do yourself a favor, and get to know a pig.

## Author's Note

I absolutely adore pigs!

I always try to keep a few handy in my kitchen pantry, ready to bring out when I have company. My guests love them!

I've included some of my most favorite pig recipes. They are not only delicious but easy-peasy!

Enjoy!

You people are INSANE!

These recipes are for figs!

FIG

## ~~PIGS~~ STUFFED WITH BLUE CHEESE

*Absolutely yummy and so simple!*

Give your pig a small pocket.
Stuff it with a half-teaspoon of blue cheese.
(Larger pigs can be stuffed with more cheese.)
*Note:* Do NOT chill the pigs. These particular pigs are tastier when kept at room temperature.

NO! NO! NO!

YUCK!

## ~~PIGS~~ IN SPICED SYRUP

*A longtime family favorite for those special holiday brunches!*

Combine ½ cup of sugar into 1 cup of water.
Simmer over low heat.
Add 1 cinnamon stick, cloves to taste, several cardamom pods, and a few allspice berries.
Grate a bit of fresh nutmeg.
Carefully place pigs in syrup.
*Note:* Don't leave pigs in syrup for an extended time, as pigs tend to become soft.
Thoroughly warm your pigs and serve.
A beautiful presentation over ice cream.

NO! NO! NO!

# PIG, FETA, AND ARUGULA PIZZA

*One of my husband's favorites. The pigs' sweetness is a perfect complement to the salty feta!*

Roll out pizza dough.

*Note:* Readily available in your grocer's freezer section.

Sprinkle with fresh pigs and crumbled feta. Bake at 375 degrees for 20–25 minutes or until cheese is melted and pigs are lightly browned. Add arugula on top.

*Buon appetito!*

FIG!

←NOPE

RIDICULOUS!

DOWN WITH PIGS

←NO!

NO! NO! BOO!!

## FRESH PIGS WITH ORANGE AND GINGER SAUCE

*A five-minute winner for a healthy treat!*

Combine and then simmer over low heat:

1 cup orange juice

1 tbsp. chopped fresh ginger

1 tsp. honey

1 star anise

Strain sauce.

Drizzle, warm, over fresh pigs.

Also available

*The Apes of Wrath*

*James and the Giant Leach*

*A Clockwork Orangutan*

*Tales from the South Pigcific*

*Pigmalion*

*Pork Chop on a Hot Tin Roof*

*Hamadeus*

*Sheepspeare Classics*

*A Tale of Two Piggies*

THE ILLUSTRATIONS IN THIS BOOK WERE MADE
WITH PHOTOSHOP, GOUACHE, AND PENCIL.

Library of Congress Cataloging-in-Publication Data

Palatini, Margie.
Under a pig tree : a history of the noble fruit / by Margie Palatini ;
illustrated by Chuck Groenink.
pages cm
On title page, the word "pig" is crossed out and replaced with "fig,"
with an explanatory note.
Summary: Using notes, an author tries to convince her publisher that her book is
about figs, not pigs, but the wording, illustrations, and even recipes present pigs as
growing on trees, and tasty with orange and ginger sauce.
ISBN 978-1-4197-1488-7
(1. Fig—Fiction. 2. Authorship—Fiction. 3. Pigs—Fiction. 4. Humorous stories.)
I. Groenink, Chuck, illustrator. II. Title.
PZ7.P1755Und 2015
(E)—dc23
2014019616

Text copyright © 2015 Margie Palatini
Illustrations copyright © 2015 Chuck Groenink

Book design by Chad W. Beckerman

Printed and bound in China
10 9 8 7 6 5 4 3 2 1

Abrams Books for Young Readers are available at special discounts when purchased
in quantity for premiums and promotions as well as fundraising or educational
use. Special editions can also be created to specification. For details, contact
specialsales@abramsbooks.com or the address below.

**ABRAMS**
THE ART OF BOOKS SINCE 1949
115 West 18th Street
New York, NY 10011
www.abramsbooks.com